THE CENTER FOR CARTOON STUDIES PRESENTS

# ANNIE · SULLIVAN
## AND · THE · TRIALS · OF
# HELEN · KELLER

BY · JOSEPH · LAMBERT

DISNEP · HYPERION BOOKS
NEW YORK

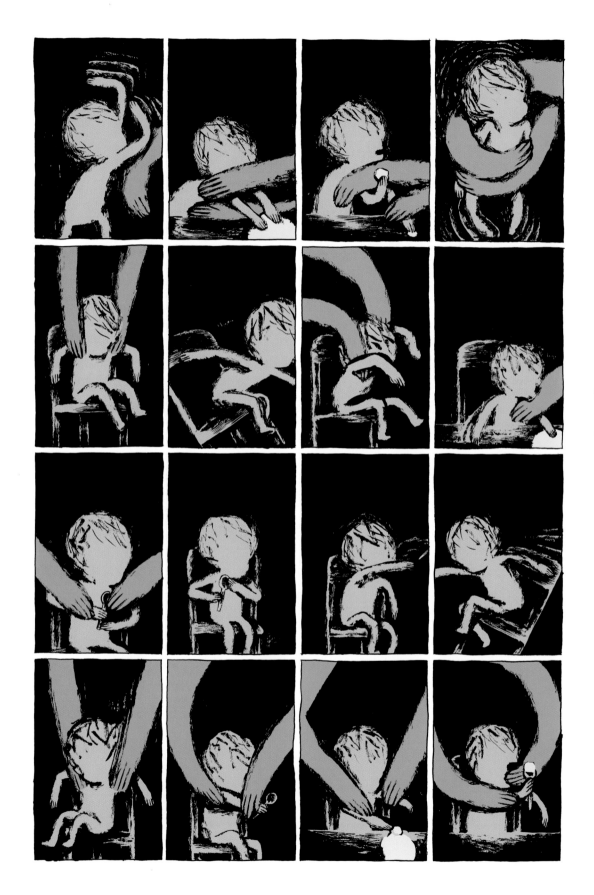

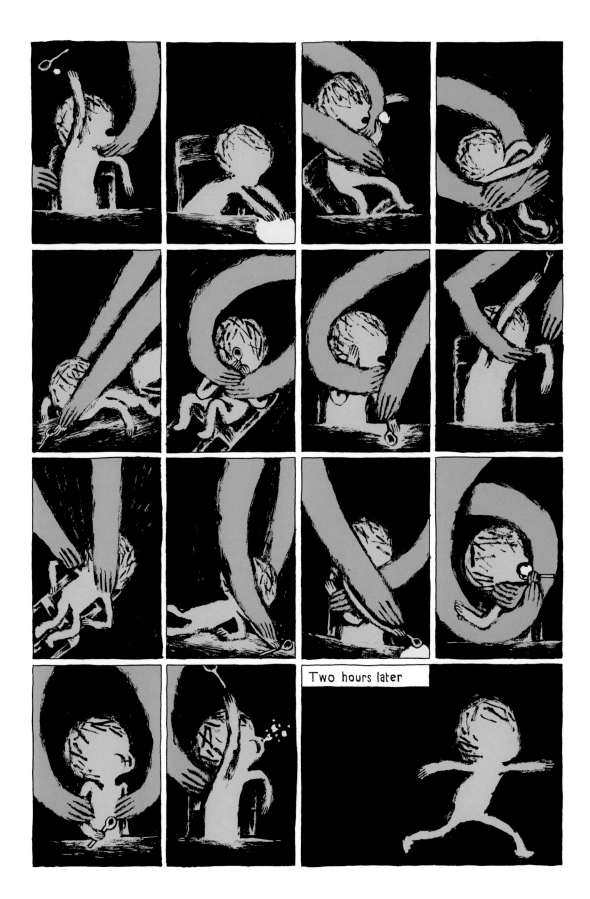

Two hours later

3

7

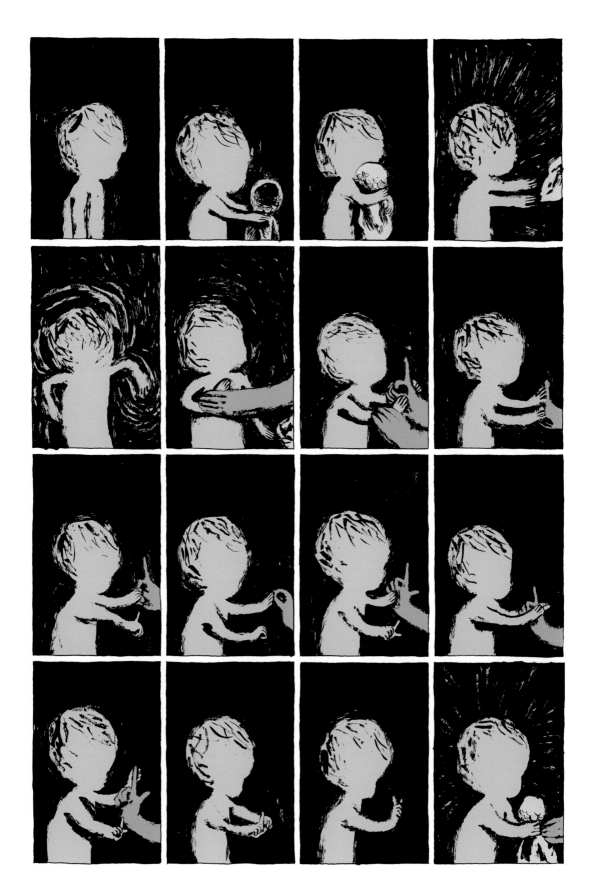

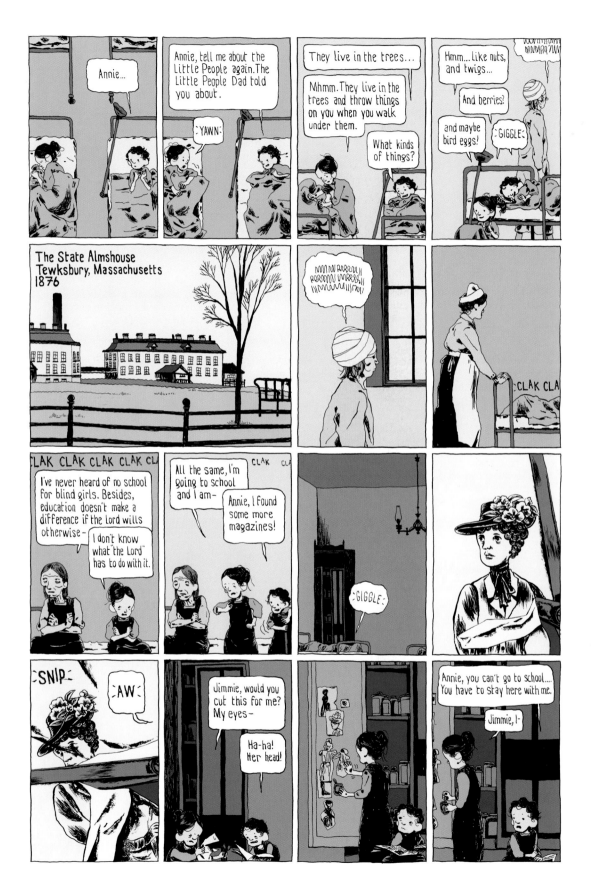

My Dear Mr. Anagnos, since I last wrote, Helen and I have gone to live by ourselves in a little, single-room garden house about a quarter-mile from the Keller homestead.

I very soon made up my mind that I could do nothing with Helen in the midst of her family,

a group who has always allowed the little tyrant to do exactly as she pleases.

≥ YAWN ≥

Captain, how many doctors have we seen? How long before we found out about Dr. Bell and Mr. Anagnos and the Perkins school?

Especially her father, who cannot bear to see her troubled.

Our meals are brought from the house and we eat on the piazza when the weather is pleasant.

How many other options do we have?

≥ SIGH ≥

The Kellers are allowed to visit every day on the condition that their presence is not made known to Helen,

and thus I have complete control over Helen, though she still refuses to let me touch her.

The first night in the garden-house she refused to sleep in the same bed as me, even though we only had the one.

I think they will have to be **responsible** for each other.

As you can imagine, I insisted

and the subsequent tussle lasted for nearly two hours.

B-E-D

P-I-L-L-O-W

Q-U-I-L-T

C-O-V-E-R

S-P-R-E-A-D

Helen has learned several nouns this week. MUG and MILK give her more trouble than others.

When she spells MILK she points to the mug and when she spells MUG she makes her sign for pouring or drinking.

To her this is still a vague game.

Ouch!

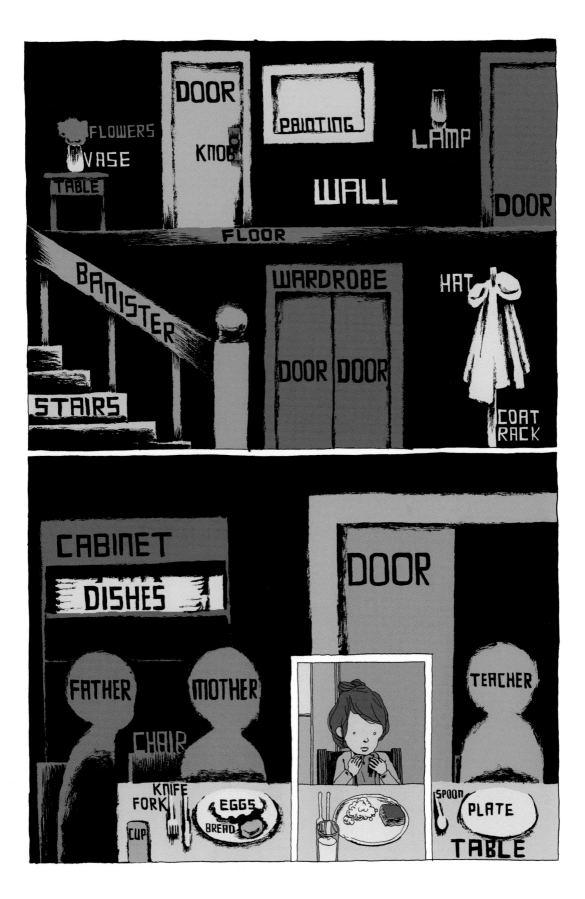

My Dear Mr. Anagnos, there is improvement in Helen day to day, almost from hour to hour.

Wherever we go she asks eagerly for the names of things. Everything must have a name now.

She drops the signs and pantomimes she used before as soon as she has the words to supply in their place.

The acquirement of a new word affords her the liveliest pleasure.

We have noticed that her face grows more expressive every day.

·NOD·

·NOD·

I have decided not to have regular lessons for the present.

Instead I treat Helen exactly like a two-year-old child.

...FLOWERS THAT SMELL LIKE HONEY...

Assuming she has the normal capacity for assimilation and imitation, I talk into her hand as one would talk into a hearing baby's ears.

SUMMER IS SEASON WITH WARM AIR AN FLOWERS WI POPPIES AND

I use complete sentences in talking to her even if a single word is all she understands.

HELEN, GIVE TEACHER SOME BREAD.

The whole sentence repeated many times will impress itself upon the brain, and by the by she will use it herself.

HELEN BREAD TEACHER

Helen knows about three hundred words now, and a great many idioms, and it is not yet three months since I have been here.

Every day we spend an hour or two poring through books, finding braille versions of words Helen already knows, and learning new ones along the way.

QUICK LITTLE FOX LEAPT OVER THE BR LOG AND INTO THE RIVER

Helen learns as many words as I can explain with the help of those she knows.

FOX

VERY FAST

QUICK

It would astonish you to see how many words she learns in this manner.

TREE

LEAVES

BRANCH

TRUNK

ROOTS

LOG

OVER

LOG

INTO

RIVER

The eagerness with which she absorbs ideas is delightful.

44

In addition to reading books, Helen and I also spend time writing.

Using the wooden, grooved writing board Dr. Bell gave us, Helen uses her forefinger to guide the tip of the pencil.

cold co
cotch
cool h
hall bo

She has taken rather quickly to writing, and takes great pleasure in it.

She is a hungry little sponge, absorbing information without bias or cynicism, and seemingly never having her fill.

OH!

-KSH-

SWEEP

I see Helen is still a little unruly hurricane.

Annie, this is my brother Frank.

Hello.

Does the little savage still dig her hands into everyone's plates?

Perhaps her nurse could watch her in another room while we have dinner in peace.

Actually, Frank, as you can see, Helen has changed quite a bit.

I suppose her cleanliness has improved.

>AHEM< Frank, our little Helen is learning to read and to write—why, just last week we had a visit from Dr. Alexander Graham Bell and w— Who?

Well, he—
Regardless, Katie, if you are happy, so am I.

Now, shall we eat? Hang this up for me, won't you Miss Abby?

Enclosed is Helen's first letter, which was written to her mother.

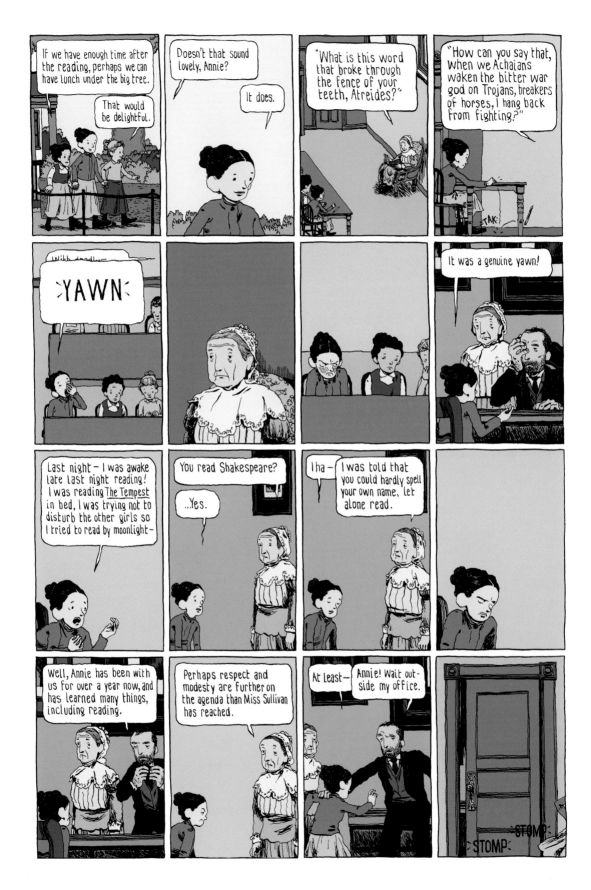

The only reason to treat Helen's curiosity about childbirth any differently is my deplorable ignorance.

It is no doubt because of this ignorance that I rushed in where the more experienced would be afraid to tread.

The only thing for me to do is to learn by making mistakes,

but in this case I do not think a mistake was made.

I drew an analogy between plant and animal—between seeds and eggs. Then I told her that certain animals and human beings don't lay eggs, but nourish the young in their own bodies.

The subject was difficult and my knowledge inadequate, but I am glad I did not dodge my responsibilities.

It is a rare privilege to watch the birth, growth, and first feeble struggles of a living mind.

This privilege is mine.

Moreover, it is given to me to rouse and guide this bright intelligence.

THE BUTTERFLY HAS BRIGHT COLOR WINGS AND THEY FL AND FLUTTER QUICKL

BUTTERFLY

I know that the education of this child will be the distinguishing event of my life,

if I have the intelligence and perseverance to accomplish it.

BUTTERFLY DOES FLY AWAY?

BUTTERFLY DOES EAT BUTTER?

Helen talks a great deal about things that she can not know about through her available senses.

THE BROWN DOG DRINKS FROM THE RIVER.

WHAT IS BROWN?

She asks about the sky, day and night, the ocean, and mountains.

BROWN IS THE COLOR OF YOUR DOG. AND THE COLOR OF EARTH, AND MUD.

SOME HORSES ARE BROWN. A TREE'S TRUNK AND BRANCHES ARE BROWN. YOUR HAIR IS BROWN TOO.

I wonder if she has any vague idea of color, any reminiscent impressions from her first nineteen months of hearing and seeing.

IS BROWN VERY PRETTY?

OF COURSE.

On the whole, her desire for knowledge is earnest and her questions never tedious, though they do draw heavily on my meager store of information. If only I were better fitted for my task....

I feel more and more inadequate every day. I need a teacher just as Helen does.

Zzz

We have borrowed books from friends and family in order to keep Helen's hunger satisfied.

Zzz

BOOK

Helen's memory is remarkable. She is able to repeat entire passages of stories verbatim after they have been read to her only once or twice, even if she does not understand every word.

Such is her capacity and desire. I hope I am capable of keeping pace.

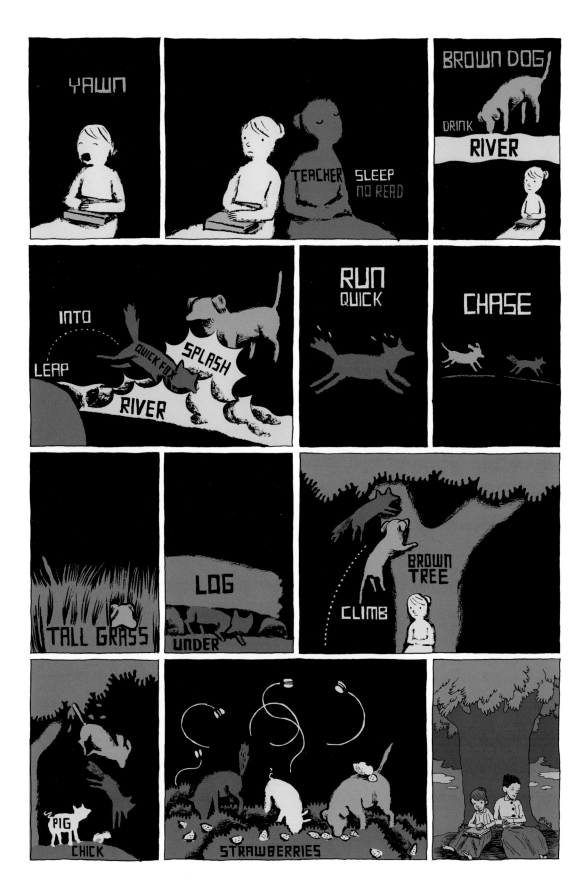

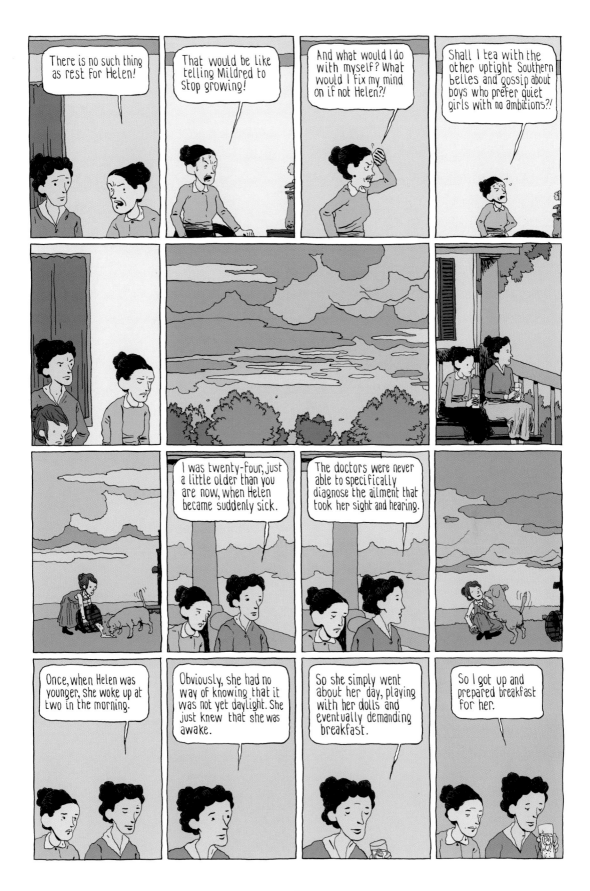

King Frost lives in a beautiful palace far to the north in the land of perpetual snow.

One day while surveying his vast wealth and thinking what good he could do with it, he had a sudden idea.

My merry fairies! I have a job for you.

I want you to deliver these to our dear friend, Santa Claus! His heart is always full of plans to benefit the poor and unhappy!

Quickly!

The fairies promised obedience, dragging the heavy jars as well as they could.

Now and then they would grumble a little at having such a hard task, for they were idle fairies and loved to play better than to work.

Now, these naughty fairies were so busy and merry over their frolic they failed to notice their hidden treasure had been spied out!

As he and King Frost could never agree as to what was the best way of benefiting the world, King Sun was very glad of a good opportunity of playing a joke upon his rival.

Hee-hee!

What could be taking them so long?

Come, North Wind, let us find those tardy couriers!

Annie and Helen are guests here and we welcome them with open arms!

What these ladies have accomplished in the field of education for the blind is a companion to what we do here at Perkins.

Perkins' founder Dr. Samuel Gridley Howe worked with Laura Bridgman, another blind-deaf girl, in a case that preceded Helen's, yes?

Indeed. In fact it is through Dr. Howe's work that Miss Sullivan had the tools for Helen's liberation, the path clearly indicated by his work with Laura.

Annie herself is Perkins educated, and of course, Helen has been continuously supported by our resources.

Our work is intertwined, one and the same! There is no resentment of any kind.

I see. Thank you.

Yes?

If your statements are true, then why continue to do these interviews? Why speak in such glowing terms about Helen?

I—

Why ask the public to read about her education when the subject has been so thoroughly exhausted by the illustrious Dr. Howe's work forty years ago?!

I see...

Annie, I understand that you want full credit for your accomplishments with Helen, but you can not deny Perkins' role.

You are often solitary, and sometimes lonely, I know. But you did not create yourself. No one does.

Nor did Perkins create itself. We owe you and Helen for the public's renewed interest in our cause.

Annie, I believe it crucial to document Helen's progress and your methods. Not only for our benefit, but also to contribute to the stock of information for those seeking knowledge.

That is why I do the interviews, why I speak in such glowing terms.

Public curiosity and intrusion upon one's privacy should be made punishable offenses.

We will just have to follow the example of little Helen herself and make the best of the inconvenience.

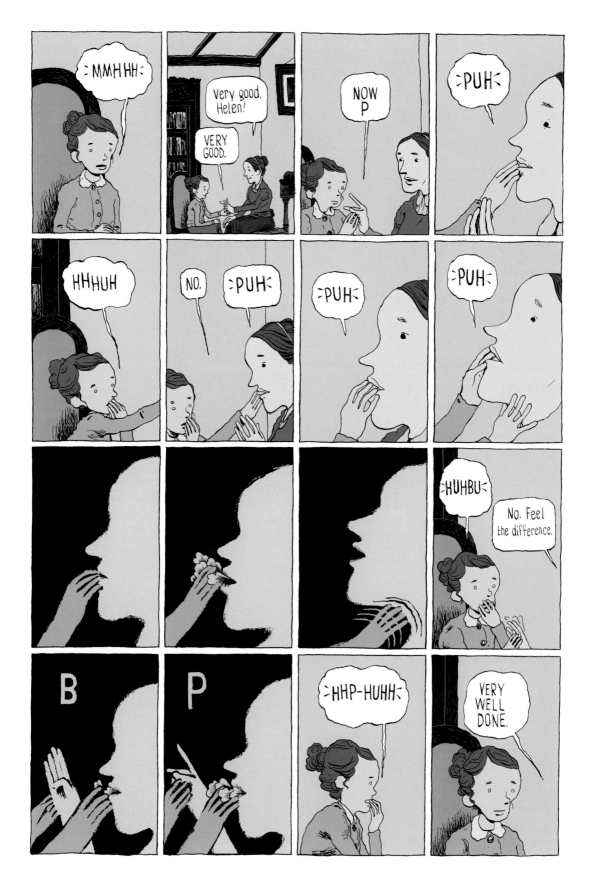

# ANNIE · SULLIVAN
## AND · THE · TRIALS · OF
# HELEN · KELLER

## *Panel Discussions*

*Page 1:* **HELEN KELLER** was born on June 27, 1880. When she was nineteen months old, she became sick with an unknown illness (now thought to have been either meningitis or scarlet fever) that left her unable to see or hear. When our story begins, Helen is not quite seven years old, has not yet attended any school, and can only communicate with her family using a few simple hand signs.

*Page 4:* **IVY GREEN** is the name of the Keller homestead in Tuscumbia, Alabama, where most of our story takes place. The house was built in 1820 by Helen's paternal grandfather, and still stands today. Visitors can explore the grounds where Helen and Annie began their lifelong friendship, and even see the water pump where Helen had the breakthrough depicted on pages 30–33.

*Page 4:* **ANNIE SULLIVAN** had a difficult childhood as the daughter of Irish immigrant farmers who lived in southwestern Massachusetts. When she was five years old, she was stricken by trachoma, an eye infection that left her nearly blind. Later, several rounds of eye surgery restored her vision to the point where she could see well enough to read. At the age of twenty, she graduated from the Perkins Institution for the Blind and moved to Alabama to tutor Helen Keller.

*Page 4:* **KATE KELLER** was Helen's mother. It was her persistence in exploring every available educational avenue that eventually led to the hiring of Annie Sullivan as Helen's governess.

*Page 4:* **ARTHUR H. KELLER**, Helen's father, was both the editor of *The North Alabamian*, a local newspaper, and owner of a small cotton plantation. He had been a captain in the Confederate Army during the Civil War.

*Page 5:* **THE CURSIVE WRITING** throughout our story is taken from journals and letters Annie Sullivan wrote in real life. We have edited certain passages to make them easier to understand. By using Annie's own words, we hope to convey as much of her personal voice as possible.

*Page 6:* **THE PERKINS INSTITUTION FOR THE BLIND** was established in 1829, when one of its cofounders, John Dix Fisher, returned to the United States after touring the first-ever school for the blind in Paris, France.

Annie Sullivan began attending the Perkins Institution in 1880, when she was fourteen. Her classmates mocked her for being an ignorant and uncivilized farm girl. Their cruelty only fueled her resolve to show them how smart she was, and she quickly became one of the top students of her class. She graduated Perkins as valedictorian in 1886, at the age of twenty.

Now known as the Perkins School for the Blind and located in Watertown, Massachusetts, the school's continuing mission is to provide assistance and education for children and adults who are blind, deaf-blind , or visually impaired.

*Page 6:* **DR. MICHAEL ANAGNOS** was director of the Perkins Institution for thirty years, from 1876 until his death in 1906. Although he is mostly remembered as the man who sent Annie Sullivan to Alabama to tutor Helen Keller, he was a prominent citizen of Boston, and had established the largest library for the blind in the world. Dr. Anagnos was a respected administrator, but his strong support of Annie Sullivan and Helen Keller was not without controversy. He promoted Helen's accomplishments in the Institution's annual report, which annoyed Annie. She believed it was a kind of bragging that created an exaggerated and unrealistic picture of Helen.

*Page 9:* **SIGN LANGUAGES** were some of the earliest means of communication created by humans. Out of necessity, Helen Keller's parents developed their own simple system of hand signs to communicate with their daughter. Annie Sullivan introduced Helen to "finger spelling," which uses individual hand signs to represent the letters of the alphabet, and combines them to spell words. Although American Sign Language (**ASL**) was standardized in the early

nineteenth century, Helen could not use it because **ASL** depends upon being able to see. However, she could eventually read and write braille, read lips by touch, type, and even speak by controlling the vibrations of her vocal cords (as seen on page 70). Helen was so passionate in her desire to communicate her thoughts and feelings that she explored every possible way to do so.

*Page 14:* **THE TEWKSBURY ALMSHOUSE** was founded in 1852 to provide food and shelter for poor immigrants, who had flocked to Massachusetts in large numbers. By 1874 it had expanded to include a hospital wing and mental health ward. The Almshouse was notoriously overcrowded, understaffed, and poorly maintained.

Annie Sullivan's mother died when Annie was eight years old, and her father, incapable of raising a family by himself, abandoned his children. Annie and her younger brother, Jimmie, were sent to the Almshouse, where Annie remained for four miserable years. In 1880, after pleading her case to a state official who was touring the grounds as part of the Tewksbury Investigations (see below), Annie was removed from Tewksbury and enrolled in the Perkins Institution for the Blind.

*Page 14:* **JIMMIE SULLIVAN,** Annie's brother, was already suffering from tuberculosis of the hip joint when he was admitted to the Tewksbury Almshouse. Tuberculosis is an often fatal infectious disease that was widespread in the nineteenth century, and continues to kill millions of people worldwide every year. Within six months of entering the Almshouse, Jimmie Sullivan had died from complications related to the disease, leaving his sister devastated and alone.

*Page 16:* **MILDRED KELLER,** Helen Keller's only sibling, was an infant when Annie Sullivan first arrived in Alabama. Due to Helen's extensive travels as an adult, the two sisters were often far apart from one another, but they remained close friends throughout their lives.

 *Page 30:* **HELEN'S BREAKTHROUGH** at the well is the most famous event in her education, having been dramatized repeatedly on stage and screen. The well itself is maintained at Ivy Green to this day, as a memorial to this turning point in Helen's life.

*Page 45:* **JULIA WARD HOWE**, though an important figure in the abolitionist and women's suffrage movements, is perhaps most well known for having written "The Battle Hymn of the Republic," a song popular during the Civil War and still sung today. She was married to Samuel Gridley Howe, a Boston doctor who cofounded the Perkins Institution for the Blind, which is why she is shown visiting and reading to the students at the school.

 *Page 45:* **THE TENNESSEE RIVER** winds through northern Alabama, at one point passing within two miles of the Kellers' home at Ivy Green. The "landing on the Tennessee" that Annie mentions here refers to a place where they could easily walk down to the water.

*Page 47:* **HELEN KELLER'S HANDWRITING** is an example of her determination to communicate with other people by any and all means within her power. After practicing diligently to draw individual letters under Annie's guidance, Helen could use the written alphabet to express her thoughts as easily as she could use the manual alphabet to finger-spell.

 *Page 56:* **THE TEWKSBURY INVESTIGATIONS** began in March 1883, after the governor of Massachusetts accused the operators of the Almshouse of misusing

funds, allowing inhabitants to starve to death in filthy surroundings, and selling the bodies of dead residents to local hospitals for research. A state legislative commission held more than thirty hearings on the matter, and within six months the managers of the Almshouse were replaced.

 *Pages 65–68:* "**THE FROST KING**" was a story written by Helen Keller when she was eleven years old and sent to Dr. Michael Anagnos, director of the Perkins Institution, as a birthday gift. Dr. Anagnos published the story in the school's alumni magazine, where it was seen as yet another of Helen's astonishing accomplishments.

It was later discovered that "The Frost King" was nearly identical to "The Frost Fairies," a story from *Birdie and His Fairy Friends*, a book published in 1889. When the similarities were made known, outsiders accused the school of deliberate deceit, and faculty members accused Annie and Helen of plagiarism. These charges led to Helen's interrogation, which lasted over two hours.

Based on the evidence, it seems clear that someone must have read "The Frost Fairies" to Helen in her early childhood, when she may have been unable to tell the difference between stories that were read to her, stories that were told to her, and things that she dreamed. She absorbed language like a sponge, and had an extraordinary memory, but the notion that a writer could "own" words may have seemed strange to her. Annie Sullivan denied ever having read "The Frost Fairies" to Helen, but Dr. Anagnos did not believe her, and felt that he could no longer trust Annie or Helen.

Regardless of how "The Frost King" came to be, the investigation into its origin was devastating for Helen. She never wrote fiction again.

*Page 69:* **LAURA BRIDGMAN** was the first deaf-blind woman to receive a substantial education in the United States. Fifty years before Helen Keller attended the Perkins Institution for the Blind, Ms. Bridgman learned how to read and write at that same school, under the tutelage of Samuel

Gridley Howe. After visiting the Institution in 1842, Charles Dickens wrote an enthusiastic appraisal of Howe's work with Ms. Bridgman in his book *American Notes*. Forty years after its publication, this piece of writing convinced Kate Keller to seek help for her daughter at Perkins.

*Page 73:* **ALEXANDER GRAHAM BELL** was an American scientist and engineer who is widely considered one of the most influential people in history. Because his mother and wife were both deaf, he devoted a significant portion of his prodigious energy to the creation of devices that could improve hearing. This led eventually to his invention of the telephone in 1875.

Bell was very active in deaf education. Like many educators of the time, he believed that all deaf people could be taught to vocalize, and that using sign language only got in the way. The glove Bell describes to Annie on page 73 was one of his many efforts to integrate deaf people into wider society. Sometimes called a "talking glove," this device had the letters of the alphabet printed on it, allowing the deaf person and anyone with whom he or she was communicating to simply spell out words by pointing at the letters. Bell hoped to make finger spelling and sign language obsolete, but his invention never caught on.

*Page 86:* **ANNIE SULLIVAN AND HELEN KELLER** became lifelong companions. When Annie died in 1936, at the age of seventy, Helen was holding her hand. After Helen died in 1968, within a few weeks of her eighty-eighth birthday, she was cremated, and her ashes were placed next to Annie's at the Washington National Cathedral in Washington, D.C.

# Bibliography & Suggested Reading

Braddy, Nella. *Anne Sullivan Macy: The Story Behind Helen Keller.* New York: Doubleday, Doran & Company Inc., 1933.

Delano, Marfe Ferguson. *Helen's Eyes: A Photobiography of Annie Sullivan, Helen Keller's Teacher.* Washington D.C.: National Geographic Society, 2008.

Garrett, Leslie. *Helen Keller: A Photographic Story of a Life.* New York: DK Publishing, 2004.

Gibson, William. *The Miracle Worker: A Play.* New York: Scribner, 2008.

Gibson, William. *Monday After the Miracle: A Play in Three Acts.* New York: Dramatists Play Service, Inc., 1983.

Herrman, Dorothy. *Helen Keller: A Life.* Chicago: The University of Chicago Press, 1998.

Keller, Helen. New York: *The Story of My Life.* Bantam Books, 1988.

Keller, Helen. *The World I Live In.* New York: New York Review Books, 2003.

Lash, Joseph P. *Helen and Teacher: The Story of Helen Keller and Anne Sullivan Macy.* New York: Delacorte Press/Seymour Lawrence, 1980.

Nielsen, Kim E. (editor). *Helen Keller: Selected Writings.* New York: New York University Press, 2005.

Sanborn, Franklin Benjamin. *Michael Anagnos, 1837–1906.* Boston: Wright and Potter Printing Co., 1907.

"Investigations. Gov. Butler's charges against the Tewksbury Almshouse management." *Lowell Weekly Sun,* Lowell, MA: March 31, 1883.

"Speech by Gov. Butler at Tewksbury's town picnic on Thursday." *Lowell Weekly Sun,* Lowell, MA: August 16, 1883.

# Credits

JOSEPH LAMBERT is the Ignatz Award–winning creator of various self-published comics. Many of these stories are reprinted in *I Will Bite You!*, a collection of his work published by Secret Acres in 2011. A graduate of The Center for Cartoon Studies, he has drawn comics and illustrations that have appeared in *Mome*, *The Best American Comics*, *Komiksfest! Review*, and *Dark Horse Presents*, as well as in *Business Week* and *Popular Mechanics*. Joseph lives in White River Junction, Vermont. Visit his Web site at www.submarinesubmarine.com.

Editor JASON LUTES lives and works in Vermont, where he teaches at The Center for Cartoon Studies. His previous books include *Houdini: The Handcuff King* and *Jar of Fools*. He is working on the third volume of *Berlin*, a graphic novel trilogy about the German city during the years of the Weimar Republic.

Series Editor JAMES STURM is the cofounder of The Center for Cartoon Studies. His previous books include *Market Day* and *Adventures in Cartooning* (with Andrew Arnold and Alexis Frederick-Frost).

Copyright © 2012 by The Center for Cartoon Studies
Publication design by Michel Vrána

Production champions:
Pat Barret and Dakota McFadzean

First Edition
10 9 8 7 6 5 4 3 2 1
F850-6835-5-11349

Printed in Singapore
Reinforced binding

Library of Congress Cataloging-in-Publication Data

Lambert, Joseph.
The Center for Cartoon Studies presents Annie Sullivan and the trials of
Helen Keller / by Joseph Lambert—1st ed.
    p. cm.
ISBN 978-1-4231-1336-2
1. Sullivan, Annie, 1866–1936. 2. Keller, Helen, 1880–1968.
3. Women—United States—Biography. 4. Women—United States—History.
5. Female friendship—United States—History. 6. Graphic novels. I. Title.
HQ1412.L34 2012
362.4'1092—dc23
[B]
2011036324

Visit www.disneyhyperionbooks.com

The Center for Cartoon Studies
P.O. Box 125
White River Junction, Vermont 05001
Visit www.cartoonstudies.org

**THE CENTER FOR CARTOON STUDIES** produces comics, zines, posters, and graphic novels (like this book about Annie Sullivan and Helen Keller!). For those interested in making comics themselves one day, The Center for Cartoon Studies is also America's finest cartooning school—offering one- and two-year courses of study, Masters of Fine Arts degrees, and summer workshops.

*White River Junction, Vermont*

VISIT WWW.CARTOONSTUDIES.ORG